I0627433

Shadows of Lucifer
A global Conspiracy

David F. Woody

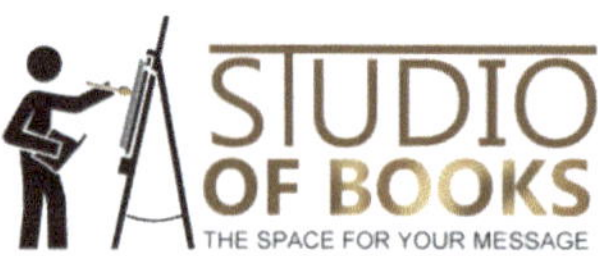

Copyright © 2024 by David F. Woody

All rights reserved. No part of this publication may be reproduced, distributed, or transmitted in any form or by any means, including photocopying, recording, or other electronic or mechanical methods, without the prior written permission of the copyright owner and the publisher, except in the case of brief quotations embodied in critical reviews and certain other noncommercial uses permitted by copyright law. For permission requests, write to the publisher, "Attention: Permissions Coordinator," to the address below.

Studio of Books LLC
5900 Balcones Drive Suite 100
Austin, Texas 78731
www.studioofbooks.org
Hotline: (254) 800-1183

Ordering Information:
Special discounts are available on quantity purchases by corporations, associations, and others. For details, contact the publisher at the address above.

Printed in the United States of America.

ISBN-13:   Softcover   978-1-964928-10-4
                       eBook: 978-1-964928-11-1

CONTENTS

Prologue

In the first story, our character David Baker, an aquatic biologist, was accosted by the Four Horsemen of the Apocalypse, who led him to Gbezx, a devil who was Lucifer's second-in-command. He took him down in a very fast elevator to Hades and a room where Lucifer, an eight-foot-tall being, was interviewing his human agents who worked for him in many different countries in the Upper World.

He was of a reddish-brown color and finely muscled, with horns much like a ram's coming out of the sides of his head above his ears. He spoke in a very pleasant voice. He convinced David to do various chores and work for him up in the Upper World, as they called it. Lucifer felt that with all the friction and wars between different countries, it would soon be time to take over Upper Earth, which had been his goal since the Garden of Eden.

Since Baker spoke French, Gbezx sent him to Quebec, Canada, to join five others a unit that passed information about local happenings down to Hades. Baker had an ongoing affair with one of the attractive young women in the group. He experienced many different exciting adventures in Quebec, Russia, and South America.

The Devil's Gambit

On the 18th hole, I had about a seven-foot putt. It looked to be straight in. If I made it, I would tie Gladoff Volsky, the Russian armorer requisitioning officer. If I missed, he would win the match. I carefully pushed the ball to the left, just missing the hole.

With a big smile, he shook my hand and said, 'Great match!'

I said in Spanish, 'I really enjoyed the game as well.'

My underworld contact, Miguel, interpreted in Russian. I speak French, Spanish, and English, but not Russian.

The four of us headed to the clubhouse for refreshments. There was Volsky, his assistant Ivan Romanoff, Miguel, and me. Miguel was assigned to me by Gbezx, who I report to. We sat down and ordered an adult beverage.

Volsky said, 'I understand that you represent a group that has interest in our new AV-1 limited nuclear weapons. It will flatten a square-mile area to the ground. It has no long-term radiation issues. It only requires two men to operate and carry it. First, we would have to be assured it only goes into the hands of people that are friendly to us.'

I said, 'I can say this my clients are a group from Iran, Yemen, Palestine, Lebanon, and Syria. I believe they are all friendly to Russia. Their target, of course, would probably be Israel. They are willing to pay a very large sum to whoever you want.'

Volsky said, 'There are many things to consider. The Americans and maybe NATO could step up, and Israel has a nuclear arsenal. This could start a worldwide nuclear war.'

We stood up, and Volsky said, 'I will contact Miguel when we can get together again.'

His change of direction kind of perplexed me.

Miguel and I went to the train station and left Peterhof Golf Club in St. Petersburg. We took a train to his home base, a building just a few miles outside the city.

Miguel said, 'Of course, the Russians have no idea that the weapons will go to Lucifer's use.'

Miguel's base was an old commercial building with about four residential apartments on the second level, occupied by his staff. One room served as a command center with their equipment. On the first floor, in one secure room, was the elevator down to Hades. The other rooms were used for storage, and one was an apartment for the security guy.

I told Miguel, 'I need to call down to Gbezx.'

Gbezx was a devil about 5'7", reddish-brown in color, with small spike horns. He was my devil contact and the second in power behind Lucifer, and I reported to him.

After a few minutes, Gbezx came to the phone, and I gave him a quick briefing. He said, 'Come down now and report all this to me and the Master, Lucifer.'

I got in the special elevator, pushed the button, and within minutes, I was in Hades.

Gbezx said, 'We will meet the Master in his office.'

Lucifer's office was very opulent, with tall ceilings and walls covered in Dutch Masters and other famous paintings. His desk was enormous, made of beautiful exotic wood. Lucifer himself was about eight feet tall with a muscular body. His skin was a brownish-red, and his horns curled out from the sides of his head, resembling a ram's. He had a very pleasant voice and a melodious laugh.

I told Lucifer what had transpired from the golf game to the meeting in the lounge.

He chuckled and said, 'I heard you are a good golfer. Clever of you to throw the game.'

I continued, 'At best, it's a maybe that we can secure the AV-1s.'

Lucifer leaned back and said, 'Let's think this through. If we arrange for some of these weapons to go to the countries that hate Israel, they will attack. Israel will have no choice but to counter with their nuclear bombs. Then, what country would they start bombing? Would the NATO nations step up? The Americans would be hesitant to intervene. This might embolden the Russians to unleash their AV-1s in Ukraine.

'This aligns with my grand plan. I want to ignite regional wars North and South Korea, China and Taiwan, India and Pakistan. China may be ready to play their high cards. The Americans will be stretched thin, trying to defend all their allies. Their economy is already fragile they could go bankrupt.

'South America is weak. If our agents fail to secure the political forces and they resist our governors and agents, my devil armies with superior weapons and knowledge could overrun all major cities in South America within weeks. The Americans, Canadians, and Australians won't even know who we are or how to find us.

'Africa is not a threat. We can leave it out of the picture for now, though our agents and my Four Horsemen are already sowing discontent. Tribal warfare is escalating, and some nations are on the brink of civil war. They will self-destruct on their own.'

Lucifer paused, then continued, 'I believe my best move now is patience. Let things simmer. We must continue to bribe corrupt officials and politicians. There is still much work to be done.'

Then he turned to me and said, 'David Baker, you will return to your base in Paris with Silvia, Mary, and the existing staff. Gbezx will give you your next assignment.'

We said our goodbyes, and I fist-bumped Lucifer. He let out a deep laugh and said, 'I bet you never thought you'd fist-bump the Devil!'

We left the room and went down the path to one of the elevators. Gbezx said, 'I'll let you settle in for a few days, then I'll call you with instructions.'

I entered the elevator, ascended quickly, and was soon in the Paris building, which was an old, vacant, closed laundry. There were two stories above the ground level. On the top floor were two two-bedroom apartments. Below, on the second floor, were three one-bedroom apartments, all of which were nicely appointed. There were also two garages connected to the laundry off the alley.

Silvia, a very attractive 35-year-old who had become my lover and oversaw the station, greeted me at the door along with her assistant, Mary. Mary, about the same age, was tall and slender. She gave me a big hug. They were still putting their things away.

Speaking French, they introduced me to the existing staff. Pierre was the security guy an ex-cop, about 5'10", thin, and fit. He was also the driver and took care of the car, which he traded every month for security reasons. Louis was the computer expert, a little overweight, about 5'8", and a jolly guy. Suzanne was the cook, a plump, friendly woman and a great gourmet chef.

The Summoning of the Horsemen

Silvia led me to my bedroom, which was one of the one-bedroom units on the top floor and next to her room. She hugged me and said she was feeling romantic, then asked me to come be with her that night.

I unpacked my suitcase and then went downstairs to the dining room. Suzanne had cooked up a nice lamb chop with delicious vegetables. After dinner, we went into the living room. Pierre uncorked a very nice bottle of red French wine, and the staff brought me up to date with what they were doing.

There was some unrest among the Muslim population, as they felt they were not being treated fairly and faced a lot of discrimination. The local French believed they were freeloaders who didn't want to work and just wanted more handouts. Crime was rising, and some of the Muslim ghettos had become so dangerous that local police wouldn't even enter the neighborhoods. The politicians now realized the mistake they had made by inviting in the immigrants. But what could they do now? Try to round them up and deport them? The hardliners said yes, while the liberals said no. So there you have it a tough conundrum.

I asked Silvia, 'Is there a group going into those areas to try to recruit some of them?'

'No,' she said. 'There doesn't seem to be a way to overcome the dogma, as they believe in Sharia law and allow no other way of thinking.

So why bother? We take our anti-Christian flyers out to some of the schools, go to protests, and talk to people. We have some contacts with the Communists, who have a large presence, as some of the higher-up politicians are socialists, along with a lot of the general population.'

Silvia then said, 'Maybe you'd like to go with Mary and Pierre to a rally tomorrow to get a feel for the land?'

I said, 'Yes, I would like that.'

Suzanne brought us all a nice glass of sherry. Everyone said their goodnights and went to their rooms. Silvia motioned for me to follow her.

Inside, she gave me a very passionate kiss, and we undressed and went to bed. As was her usual, when we finished, she said, 'Thanks,' rolled over, said, 'Good night,' and went to sleep.

Well, so much for that, I thought. So, I got dressed and went to my room.

The next day, I joined Pierre and Mary in the old Toyota. Pierre drove to the area where the protesting was taking shape, and we parked a few blocks away before walking over to see what was happening. Pierre recognized one of the protesters, went over to talk to him, and then brought him over to meet us.

His name was Mohammed, and he was somewhat of an organizer for the Muslim group. He also knew some of the Communists who wanted to spread their dogma and recruit more followers to their cause. He asked what we were doing there, and Pierre explained, 'We are part of an anti-Christian order, so our goals are pretty much the same as yours.'

Mohammed looked a bit suspicious of us, so Mary handed him one of our flyers. He said he didn't speak or read French, so Mary read it to him. She also gave him a few flyers to distribute among his people. He said, 'We will no doubt run into each other in the future, and once I get to trust you, I will invite you into our circle and introduce you to some of our leaders.' Then, he went back to join his group.

I didn't like or trust him, but I remembered what one of my mentors had said many years ago 'You don't have to like someone to do business with them.'

Mary said, 'He would be good to develop as an agent for our cause.'

We walked around the perimeter and handed out more flyers. At that moment, the police showed up, so we made a hasty retreat.

When we returned to home base, Silvia told me to call Gbezx. He instructed me to return to the Underworld the next day.

I took the fast elevator and was soon in Hades. I met Gbezx, and we walked down the path to a large room, maybe 40 feet wide and 60 feet long. A large table sat in the center, seating about 30 people. The walls were covered with large Upper World maps. There were two open seats, which Gbezx and I took. Gbezx explained that the rest of the seats were occupied by their human agents governors from all over the Upper World.

We were all given earphones that translated the different languages.

A few minutes later, Lucifer entered the room, holding a pointer in his hand. He was over eight feet tall, and with his dominating presence, he easily commanded the room. He moved to each map and described the condition of every country as he went around.

He explained, 'Each agent must prepare for the eventual collapse of the local governments as the Upper World nuclear Armageddon unfolds in their region. My advisors will send plans and further information as we move forward. These will be very hectic times for all of you governors. As you know, I have waited thousands of years for this perfect storm to aid me in my domination of the Upper World.

'The key will be how we handle the political situation, as the fighting and devastation will be influenced by the people of the Upper World. We are currently training many politically savvy individuals to assist you. You will receive detailed instructions on how to shield yourselves and your staff from radiation and what precautions to take.'

Then, he asked if there were any questions. Several hands went up. Each person spoke in their language, and Lucifer responded in the same tongue he spoke all the languages of the Upper World. The translations came through our earphones.

This continued for several hours.

The meeting broke up, and everyone left the room to go back to their assigned countries. I went back to the elevator and up to Paris. The next day, I got a call from Gbezx. He said there was a big problem brewing in the unit in Buenos Aires and for me to catch a plane that they had made reservations for out of Paris in 2 hours.

After the long flight, I landed, took a taxi, and went directly to the unit about a block away. I went up the alley and entered a secret door at the rear of the building. The Control agent, Carlos, met me and said Gbezx had told him I was coming and that I should take over. He took me into the front room, and looking out on the front lawn were several protestors with signs yelling, "Kill the Satanists and Devil worshippers." The crowd parted and began cheering as ten or twelve Templar Knights in full armor came out of a bus. Their shields, with Maltex crosses on them, came walking through the crowd and up to the front door, which was fortunately reinforced steel. They began yelling for the people to come out, pulled their long two-handled swords from their scabbards on their backs, and began chopping at the door and the windows.

I ran out the back door, jumped the five-foot neighbor's block wall to the right of the mayhem, and huddled down. I had my special phone and called Gbezx, telling him I needed the Four Horsemen of the Apocalypse right now. In less than ten minutes, they all appeared astride their fearsome horses in black chrome armor. There was the demon of Pestilence, War, Famine, and Death, who I had met before. They were behind the Knights, who were busy chopping at the door and windows. The Horsemen unsheathed their swords and attacked the Knights.

Behind the Horsemen, the local cops showed up but were afraid of firing so as not to kill the Knights. The fighting and the clashing of swords against armor, the cursing and yelling, were deafening. The Horsemen pushed forward, but the well-trained Knights pushed them back a few feet. One of the Knights fell with an arm wound, and two others went down with serious wounds. The fighting and cursing were tremendous.

The Knights loudly yelled, "We are the protectors of Christ, we are the righteous. Our order is sacred, death to the non-believers."

The Knights could not inflict any damage on the Horsemen no matter how hard and bravely they fought, even though they outnumbered them three to one. The leader of the Knights yelled out to his comrades, "We need to leave now as the Demons are unkillable. Pick up the wounded, and let's all leave and get to the bus."

The Horsemen reined in their steeds and pulled to the side. The Knights picked up their wounded and made it to the bus, and then it pulled away. Once the Knights were safe on their way on the bus, they began to wonder what they had encountered. The leader said they had to be demons from Hell, as no one else could have survived their onslaught, and the people in the house were part of it. "We must destroy them after the Demons on horseback leave," he said. They all agreed.

The cops and militia began a tremendous barrage of gunshots and machine gunfire at the Horsemen, to no avail. I called Gbezx and told him it was over. The Horsemen made a few steps forward and then disappeared. The cops were flabbergasted and looked at each other in disbelief. They had never encountered anything like this and decided the wise thing for them to do was to pull back and assess the situation and be ready to get out of there in case they came back.

I hurried back into the house and told Jean, 'They must all leave now.' He said they had evacuation plans and knew where to go. They quickly packed their gear and clothes, and we went to the attached garage, loading up into two vans. Fortunately, all the police were still in front and hadn't come around to the back.

I called Gbezx, and he told me to fly back to Paris temporarily. He said he would close the elevator after sending a team to set fire to and destroy the small commercial building.

No Regrets, No Remorse

I took the first plane I could for the long trip from Buenos Aires to France. I went to meet the team in Paris at my home base. I joined our group for a couple of adult beverages and told them about the adventure in Buenos Aires and how having steel-reinforced doors and windows saved the team there. We all decided we had better reinforce this property. Who could we hire as a contractor, or should we do it ourselves? I suggested I contact Gbezx and get his guidance. They all agreed that for security reasons, that would be best.

They said, 'Now we have a scary story to tell.' Last time, they were out putting out flyers, and Mohammed and an accomplice were following Silvia and Mary, who are both old pros at shaking off tails. They both carry small .38 caliber automatic pistols in their purses.

Silvia called Pierre on her cell phone and told him the situation. He said he would drive around for a few blocks, doubling back, and then stop, get out of the car, and watch to see if anyone was following. Silvia and Mary split up, and Silvia went into a department store. She stood to the side up front to see if anyone showed up, then went to the back and exited the store or just went back out the front if the followers went in. Mary walked across the street, going the opposite way she was going for a while, then got behind a tree to see what their pursuers were doing.

Pierre called them both and said he would pick them up at the corner of 6th St and 8th Ave. He said that if the pursuers were still following them on foot, they would, of course, be outdistanced from them in the car. 'If they do get their license number, it won't matter,' he said, 'as I take plates off other cars, which I do frequently as soon as I get another car. I also trade the car off to a crooked used car dealer who changes cars every two weeks or so for security reasons. I told the dealer it's an ongoing college/gas company experiment we're performing.'

Pierre drove for a few blocks and then pulled over to the curb so they could see if there were any followers. He went to the trunk of the car, got another plate, and his battery-powered drill motor, quickly changing the plates. The Department of Motor Vehicles requires that you must have a front and back plate, so Pierre takes the front plates, which is probably not noticed by most drivers or the cops.

They waited for 20 minutes, then proceeded to come back to their base, circling around a couple of times. I said, 'They did good.' We all started talking and wondering what Mohammed was up to. It couldn't be good, as if he wanted to talk, he would have done so at the rallies or protests.

We all checked to make sure we didn't have his phone number in our phones, and Silvia asked, 'Did we give him ours?' Except for Silvia and I, the rest had throwaway cell phones.

'The French government is secretly deporting some of the Muslim troublemakers,' I said. 'Maybe he thinks we are agents of The Police Nationale or Gendarmerie.'

Meanwhile, I got a call from Gbezx. It seems that in Baltimore, Maryland, in the U.S., a woman member of a white supremacist group had just been sentenced to 18 years for plotting to destroy electrical facilities in Baltimore to destabilize the area. Gbezx said I should go to Baltimore and see if there are any opportunities to recruit from the supremacist group after we resolve the issue with Mohammed.

Our group decided that we could not trust Mohammed, and we wondered what his game was. There was another protest this coming Friday evening, and the news said it was going to be attended by some of the Muslim groups. Pierre said maybe a couple of us should disguise ourselves as Muslims and see if we could spot Mohammed and try to tail him.

Pierre and I went to the Muslim district the next day, where there are several shops, and we bought some long robes and head covers at a shop where the proprietor spoke French. He was very helpful dressing us up, including sandals. We told him we were going to a party of one of our Muslim friends and wanted to surprise him. I also bought a Koran to carry at the protest.

On Friday afternoon, Pierre and I, all dressed up in our new garb, parked the car we had just bought about 4 or 5 blocks away and walked up toward the groups that were starting to form. People were just talking to each other, and some were handing out signs. I asked for a sign, and we walked around through the crowd hoping we would spot Mohammed.

Pierre said he thought he recognized one of the guys who was with Mohammed at the other protest. We followed him, and he stopped. We stopped and looked the other way. He was looking around, and in a few minutes, Mohammed showed up and greeted him. The crowd had grown and was getting a little rowdy, with lots of yelling and flag-waving. The Gendarmerie showed up in riot gear in front of the protesters.

We were getting a little nervous, so we kind of shuffled back into the middle, trying to keep an eye on our prey. There was a surge forward by the crowd, and the police began hitting them with their batons and throwing tear gas canisters in the middle. The new current political party had promised to really crack down on the protesters. We could see down the street about two to three hundred National Guard and Army troops advancing toward us with fixed bayonets on their rifles.

Pierre said, 'Let's get the hell out of here,' so we pushed and slugged our way to the back of the melee, which was a hell of a chore.

We decided to take off our headgear and robes so we wouldn't be mistaken for some of the Muslims. As luck would have it, we bumped into Mohammed and his associate at a distance. He yelled to us to follow him over to the right so we could talk. There were a lot of people coming back through, trying to get away from the police. Pierre yelled at me that he had a bad feeling about this and suggested we go to the left and get to the car. We ran and jostled through the crowd, losing sight of Mohammed.

We got to the car and got in, with me in the passenger seat and Pierre on the driver's side. My window was up, and I locked the door.

Pierre's window was down, and in that instant, Mohammed reached in the open window, grabbed Pierre's hair with his right hand, pulled his head back, and put a large knife to his throat. He said, 'You dirty infidel spies have breathed your last.'

I had put a Ruger .357 Magnum revolver in the glove box, which I took out. Seeing no choice, I shot Mohammed in the forehead, and I told Pierre to roll his window up. Two of Mohammed's accomplices were hammering on the windows. I opened my window, showed one of them the gun, and told him to back off or I would shoot him as well.

Pierre then started the car, and we pulled away. I looked back to see three of them attending to Mohammed. The road was cluttered with people and a few cars, so our progress was slow. I told Pierre, 'You don't take a knife to a gunfight,' and we both shared a nervous laugh.

I've never killed anyone, and I told Pierre how I was feeling. He said, 'You saved my life and totally did the right thing, so be easy on yourself. You will no doubt have regrets that you might suffer in the future. When the regrets come to visit you, just close the door to them and say goodbye.'

After we had driven for a distance, Pierre pulled over to the side of the road, opened the trunk, took out a license plate that was off another car, took the existing one off, and screwed in the new plate.

Pierre said he would trade in the car tomorrow to the crooked car dealer he dealt with. He changes cars every month and sooner if an episode comes up like today. He buys cheap, older cars that are dependable but maybe not in the best shape on the exterior.

We went back to our base and joined the others. Over a couple of nice French wines, we told the rest about our adventures of the day. The line of thinking was that we needed to stay away from the Muslims. Suzanne had prepared a pot roast with a lot of nice vegetables. Louis had bought three nice bottles of French wine from a friend who worked in a local wine shop, which went very well with the meal.

Whispers of War and Shadows of Deception

I received a call from Gbezx, and he told me to come down to the underworld the next day as he had a new assignment for me. As I got off the elevator, there was a large, winged devil waiting for me, who motioned me to get on his back. We took off down the pathway for about a mile and a half, and I was dropped off at Gbezx's office. It was kind of fun riding on the devil's back.

I went in, and there were two other humans sitting across from Gbezx. He introduced them as agents from Israel, Seth and Abraham. Their idea was to induce Israel to attack the air bases and suspected nuclear facilities in Iran. This would stir up the Iranians to enlist their allies in the region Syria, Lebanon, Palestine, maybe Jordan and make a combined attack on Israel. And so, you know, there's a lot of resistance from certain religious factions in Israel not to expand the fighting. We are working on that problem now.

Seth said that Gbezx had told them I had a friend in the Israeli military intelligence who was hawkish, and with some monetary persuasion (perhaps a few handfuls of gold 1oz Canadian Maple Leaf coins) and claims of cooperation with the U.S., maybe he could get their high command to go for the attack on Iran. Abraham said this would put a lot of pressure on the U.S. leaders to enter the fray and put boots on the ground.

I asked them what Yemen might do. Seth said Saudi Arabia may have to deal with them, so it may not have an immediate effect. Besides, some of the European nations have warships patrolling the Red Sea and the Gulf of Aden. Abraham said he thought this would be a good start if I'm willing to try it. He said that he and Seth haven't had any luck reaching the right people. Security is very tight. He knew it would be dangerous, as I could be arrested as a foreign spy, and my friend might not be able to help me. The Mossad, who are the Israeli secret police, don't believe in trials. They arrest you, take you out, and bury you in the desert.

They told me they would provide a room for me and a car with a driver. I said I'd be willing to see how it goes. Seth said, "You can go up in the elevator with us, and we'll get you settled in your room and introduce you to your driver."

Gbezx said to go to the treasury and get some gold coins and some shekels, then head to the clothing facility. Seth and Abraham could pick out what clothes would be appropriate. I exchanged phone numbers with them. They said to speak English and to be a reporter for a small TV station, and I could get my ID and some notepads from the facility.

Gbezx took me to the side and said, "There are other opportunities beginning to crop up in other parts of the world that we need to think about. If you can't make any progress right away, then come back. Good luck, and report when you can."

Seth, Abraham, and I boarded the elevator and soon ended up in a small room in Haifa, Israel. It was behind a small shop that the agents owned and operated. They sold shoes and clothing, and there were several kinds of shops on the street. Seth called the driver, who came by and picked us up. We went to a small two-story apartment building where Seth, his wife Rachael, and their children lived. Abraham lived in another part of town, and he left us.

They had set up a small room for me. It was dinner time, and Rachael cooked lamb with some nice vegetables that were very tasty. After dinner, we went out on the second-floor balcony, smoked a nice Cuban cigar, and had a glass of brandy. We chatted about Lucifer's plan to take over the world. He said he was an atheist and belonged to a group that met once a week for breakfast.

There was a shared bathroom and shower, so they told me, as the guest, I could go first. My bunk was small but comfortable.

The next morning, after breakfast, the driver came, and Seth and I got aboard. We drove out to the military facility where I believed my friend had his office. I got out of the car and walked about four or five blocks to the security gate.

I showed my ID and told the guard I was here to see an old friend in Mossad. He told me to come in and wait in a small room with a table and three chairs. After about an hour, an officer came in, frisked me, and then sat across the table from me. He said his name wasn't important and that I could call him Captain.

"What is your name?"

"David Baker," I said.

"What is your friend's name?"

"Benjamin Cohen."

"What is your purpose for being here?"

"I'm here to see an old friend."

"Where did you meet him?"

"It was at a conference of security and intelligence officers in Toronto, Canada."

"When was that?"

"About 15 years ago."

"What did you do, and what was your position?"

"I was an intelligence officer with the Security Department of Toronto."

"You came all this way to just see a friend?"

"I've never been here, and I wanted to see all the religious sites."

"Are you religious?"

"No, not really."

"Ok," he said, "I guess you're ok. We can't take any chances, as you know. I'll call Major Cohen to let him know you're here."

The captain had me follow him to a two-story grey stucco building that had several office suites inside. We walked up the stairs, went down the hall past a number of noisy offices, to a door that the captain knocked on. An enlisted female soldier opened it and asked what we wanted. He told her I wanted to see the Major. She said, "Okay, come in," and the captain left us.

The Major got up, and we shook hands. He led me to his office at the back. It was maybe 15 square feet, with a desk, three chairs, and was fairly sparse.

I said, "Man, it's been a long time."

He replied, "Yes, it has. Well, let's get to business."

I told him, "It's in my client's interest that Israel attacks the airbases, oil fields, and any nuclear buildings, if possible, in Iran. I wasn't told, so I can only speculate on the reasoning—maybe something to do with oil, money, and politics."

I continued, "This will be good for Israel to stem the rocket attacks and wipe out Iran's source of income from oil revenues to hamper the support they give to terrorist groups. My clients will pay you and your military service handsomely."

"Well, yes, that's in line with my thinking," he said. "However, it will be very difficult for a number of reasons:

Our people will worry about the U.S. response.

Other countries such as Turkey, Iraq, the Saudis may get nervous.

We also have antiwar factions here.

I do think we will have enough hawks in the higher echelons who would be receptive to your plan."

I said, "I have 10 one-ounce gold coins I could give you as a good faith deposit, if you want. Also, my clients will deposit $100,000 or more in a Cayman Islands bank or your choice of bank to each of the people who help us with this mission."

"Well," Cohen said, "let me talk to one of my friends who has a lot of influence and is friends with some of our top generals. We'll need to go slowly with this, so we don't make any slip-ups. It was so good seeing you again. Let's exchange phone numbers."

With that, I said, "Good luck, and we'll see what happens," and I was escorted out of the compound and walked down to the car. I told Abraham and Seth what had happened. We went back to the apartment, and I called Gbezx. He said, "It will be a waiting game for now, so have Seth and Abraham continue with their work and for you to come back to the underworld."

I met Gbezx at his office, which I loved seeing as he had old Dutch Masters on the walls, which I really enjoyed. He had exquisite furnishings with antique furniture, and next to the chair I sat in was a large old pirate treasure chest he said came from the pirate Blackbeard's hoard, full of gold, silver coins, and chains.

"How did you find it?" I asked.

Gbezx said, "One of our agents in the Caribbean had heard about the wreck, and we financed an exploration venture. They found the shipwreck and recovered the entire fortune."

"How did they divide it up?" I asked.

"It was appraised, and the divers and boat crew received a handsome share, as well as our agent who gave it to his friends and family."

I reached in and pulled out a handful of silver 'pieces of eight' and thought out loud, "Wow, these coins must be over 200 years old."

Gbezx said, "As you can imagine, they don't mean much to me, but as you enjoyed running them through your fingers, some of my other visitors do the same."

Gbezx continued, "When we ran your top-secret information profile before we brought you in, I didn't see where it noted that you were an intelligence officer in the Quebec secret service."

I said, "That's a lie I just came up with to make the captain let me in to see Major Cohen. I was hoping he wouldn't check it out."

"Okay, that was good. You lucked out," Gbezx said.

Gbezx said, "So we have a waiting game for the Mossad Major to make his contacts. We have the Russians contemplating selling us the AV-1 Limited Nuclear Weapon. So, while we wait, I want you to go to Madrid, Spain. As you also speak Spanish, you'll be able to travel around with little problems.

We have a situation where one of our agents, Sally, has been arrested by the Centro Nacional de Inteligencia, the Spanish Intelligence agency. She is being held in one of their prisoner holding cells. One of our agents, Ricardo, is a cook who works there. He delivers food to the prisoners, and he said they've been torturing her, and she is begging him to give her some poison.

Gbezx said his idea was for me to go to Ricardo's apartment and give him a poison pill to give to her in her food. "You'll need to be extremely careful, as the agency will do spot checks on the employees. We will set up a breakfast meeting for you and Ricardo to meet, and you'll give him the pill. Ricardo goes to a certain restaurant every morning. We'll tell him that you'll come by his table without looking at him and drop the pill on a napkin by his plate. Then you'll go to the restroom at the back of the room, exit out the front, and maybe one other time go to the counter for a cup of coffee."

"It might be wise to watch the restaurant for a couple of days, walk in, and go by his table as a dry run. Don't leave the pill until you feel it's safe. We'll tell him the second time you'll drop the poison."

"How does that sound to you?" he asked.

"It sounds like a well-thought-out plan," I said. "Too bad Sally must die."

"Yes, but there's no way to get into the facility, and we need to relieve her suffering."

"Go down to the supply room and get Spanish-style clothes, Spanish Pesos, ID, passport, and the poison pill, maybe three in case you lose one, and your plane tickets."

We said our goodbyes, and I hitched a ride on one of the devils and went to the supply room. From there, I took the elevator to my home base in France.

Two days later, Gbezx called to say everything was set up for the meeting with Ricardo. I was to meet Pierre, who took me to the airport. My trip to Madrid in 1st class was enjoyable, and I had fun flirting with one of the pretty stewardesses. I took a taxi to my hotel, went to the bar, and ordered three fingers of red whiskey in honor of my old Russian friend, Boris. After a great Spanish breakfast, I took a taxi to the address of the restaurant where Ricardo would be. I told the driver to wait, as I would be right back.

I went in, and it had about five tables on the left that would hold four people. On the right were four small tables that would hold two. A small bar was also on the right. Ricardo would be at the last table on the right and would wear a yellow baseball cap. The place was about half full of patrons. I went down to the end, turned around, and came back to the front, telling the hostess I was looking for a friend. Then I went back to the cab and returned to my hotel room.

The next morning, I went back to the restaurant, and to the back, Ricardo was at the last table and was wearing a yellow cap. I went down the aisle about ten feet from him, winked, and he winked back. I left in my cab and asked the driver to take me on a trip around the city, which he was happy to do, as I offered him a nice fee.

The next morning was the same, except it was the drop-off day. I wrapped the pill in a small piece of toilet paper and put it in my right jacket pocket. I took a different cab to the restaurant, telling the cabbie to wait. I went in, and only a few customers were there. I went by his table and dropped off the pill on the napkin he had laid there. I walked into the restroom, waited a few minutes, came back out, and Ricardo had removed the pill. I walked out the front door.

"Perfect," I thought. "Piece of cake!" Ricardo left about the same time I did, and Gbezx reassigned him to another station in Argentina. I heard he made it okay. I had my personal effects, so I had the cabbie take me straight to Madrid Barajas Airport, and I flew to Paris, France.

I went to the office to see the rest of my roommates, and Suzanne said to wash up as she was getting dinner ready. The meat was Osso Buco in a nice sauce and a tasty assortment of vegetables. I told them about my adventure in Spain, and they were shocked to hear about Sally, who Mary had met at a meeting some time ago.

Silvia asked, "Wasn't there something else we could have done, like a prisoner exchange or something?"

"Well," I said, "there was no practical way to gain entrance to the heavily guarded compound, and they would torture her and then kill her no matter what we tried."

I asked, "What has happened about the episode we had with Mohammed and his followers?"

"It was all in the papers and on the TV news," Mary said. "One of the followers had gotten the license number of our car, and they found out it was off a lady schoolteacher's car. She hadn't even realized it was missing, and she was in France on a visit with her husband in his car at the time. The husband is a city official and well known. Pierre had switched the plates the day before. Lucky thing for us."

"What do the authorities think the incident was all about?" I asked.

Mary said, "As you can imagine, there are all kinds of theories going around, from a drug deal gone bad to some kind of political doings. The conservatives say now is the time to start expelling the Muslims. The liberals say that's not the right thing to do, and the Catholic Church said they are God's children, and we need to take care of them."

I said, "We might want to lay low and stay away from any protest by the Muslims or otherwise."

Gbezx called and told me to come down as Lucifer wanted to see me. I took the elevator down and went to his office, and we both went to Lucifer's office. There were the two Israelis, Seth and Abraham, that I had worked with. We all said our hellos.

Lucifer said, "It looks like the Israelis have saved us the trouble of going through the Mossad Major to induce his superiors to bomb Iran and Syria. However, we need to continue to stir up the pot in the area."

Seth said, "His contacts in Turkey tell him the Turks are getting nervous about the fighting in Lebanon between Hamas and the Israelis. Iran is funding several of the terrorist groups from Yemen to Damascus, which is very concerning to them."

"Ok," Lucifer said, "Seth and Abraham, I want you to go back to your base in Haifa and see what new intelligence you can find in that area, particularly Turkey. We have a good agent in Istanbul we will connect you with, and you will need to meet with him. Gbezx will set it up, so go ahead and leave us now, please."

After they had left, Lucifer said, "David, we want you to go up to St. Petersburg and meet with Miguel. Maybe you can set up another golf game with Volsky to find out about us being able to purchase their new AV-1 mobile nuclear weapon." Laughing, he said, "And be sure to let him win the round like you did on your last game. What is your handicap?"

"About three or four," I said.

"And what is Volsky's?"

"I think he said about fifteen."

"Well, you should have no trouble making the match interesting."

"Ok," I said as I got up, and Gbezx and I left his office.

Gbezx said, "Why don't you go back to your base in France for a couple of days, and when Miguel has the meeting with the Russian set up, I will contact you, and you can go meet him."

I took the fast elevator up to my base in Paris and was just in time for dinner. I shook hands with Pierre and Louis and got hugs from Mary, Silvia, and Suzette. Suzette had cooked up a wonderful beef stew with sourdough bread. Pierre had bought a couple of bottles of very nice red wine. They all told me it was a little bit boring without me here to create an adventure for them. They go to meetings and hand out anti-Christian flyers and have been chased out of a few places. They have a couple of new recruits that are promising.

I told them I've been going around the world on various assignments. I said I will need to leave in a few days again; I'm just waiting for the order. I asked if anything else had happened since our affair with Mohammed.

Pierre said that whole thing simmered down and guessed it's because it was a Muslim that got killed. Pierre said he had found a different car dealer to make sure that the lead was not followed. They said they had been going to several of the tourist sites in Paris and how cool they were. They also go to some of the sidewalk cafés that are fun.

After a couple of cocktails, everyone went to bed. Silvia winked and went to her room. I went to mine and waited for a few minutes, then went to hers. I joined her in bed, and we made passionate love. Afterward, when we were through, she asked me if I had any thoughts about us getting married.

I said, "Well, er, ah, no, I haven't, but it will be on my mind as you are the perfect woman for me."

She said, "Well, I guess that's better than nothing."

I headed back to my room and fell asleep right away.

Echoes in the Shadow

The next morning, we had a great breakfast of poached eggs, French sausages, and baked tomatoes. Silvia wanted to go back to the Louvre, so she, Mary, and I, with Pierre driving, went around for a while through the streets of Paris. We then parked and went to the Louvre, where we saw the Mona Lisa and Winged Victory, amongst other attractions. Amazing artworks.

We went to a nice sidewalk café for lunch, and Pierre elbowed me as down the sidewalk came who we thought might be one of Mohammad's friends that was at the car when I shot Mohammad. We both turned our heads, and the person walked on by. We waited until he was down the street a ways, and then we told the ladies we had to get out of there quickly. Our car was parked down the street a block in the opposite direction from where the guy was walking, fortunate for us. We hurried back to our building and stopped about two blocks away. I took the .38 caliber pistol out of the glove box, got out of the car, and told Pierre to go around the back and park in our garage.

I waited by a big tree next to the sidewalk to see if anyone followed us. After about a half hour, I walked to the building and went in the back door off of the alley. I joined the rest in the living room, and we were lamenting the fact that we had some bad luck with our dealings with the Muslims. It might not have been an associate of Mohammad's, but he seemed to resemble him.

"We'll all really have to be alert of our surroundings, as they can recognize David and Pierre," Silvia said. "We also need to follow up with Gbezx regarding reinforcing the door and first-floor windows in case the Knights Templar come knocking."

I said, "I think heavy wrought iron bars may do the trick."

Louis opened a nice bottle of brandy and passed it around. Suzanne called us to dinner, and she served pork chops, candied yams, pickled beets, and a nice fresh French bagel with butter and orange marmalade. "Veilleux!"

Gbezx called and gave me ticket info that was arranged for me to fly to Moscow and to pick up my tickets at the counter at the airport in 2 hours. Pierre drove me in heavy traffic and dropped me off with no problems. I wore dark glasses and a baseball cap to pass through, hoping not to see any of the bunch that had attacked us in the car. Miguel met me at Vnukovo Airport in Moscow, and we went to his home base. Speaking Spanish, he said he had a golf date set up for us the next day at 9:00 AM.

I stayed the night in Miguel's guest room, and the next day we drove out to Peterhof Golf Course. It was not as well-groomed or laid out as the golf courses we play in the West. We met Volsky at the rather sparse clubhouse. I had to rent clubs, and Volsky had his own. Miguel and Ivan caddied for us. As we played along, I kept pace with him. He would get a birdie, I would also. He made a par, and I would too. On the 17th hole, I made a bogey and he pared, so I was 1 hole behind him. On the 18th and final hole, he made a bogey and so did I, so he won the match with an 87 and was very pleased. He said, "I think you are a better golfer than you played today!" I said, "I have my ups and downs, and I normally shoot in the low 90's."

The four of us went to the uninspired bar for an adult beverage. He said, "I have bad news for you. Putin and one of his generals said no deal for the AV-1 sale."

"Well, you gave it a good try," I said. We said our goodbyes, and Miguel and I left. He took me to the airport, and I flew back to Paris. Pierre picked me up, and he brought me up to date.

It seems that Israel has made another attack on the air force bases and bunkers in Iran, and this is really stirring the pot in the Middle East. The Israelis told the Iranians if they didn't release the hostages and stop the rocket attacks, they would bomb the nuclear facilities and maybe use a limited atomic bomb. The NATO members called for an emergency meeting, and many of the other world leaders, including U.S. President Biden, will attend at the United Nations building.

Russia has sent a large flight of bombers to Ukraine and hit their military bases and some of the cities. It is total chaos. The U.S. is really taken aback and not sure what to do. U.S. President Biden had stated that the U.S. is behind the Ukrainians; however, this is a new development. The Chinese are massing their military, maybe to make a move on Taiwan, as speculation is that the U.S. and NATO will be tied up elsewhere. They consider the U.S. president in a weakened position, so now may be the time.

The Hutias in Yemen are stepping up their attacks on shipping in the Red Sea and the Gulf of Aden. Britain and France are sending warships, including aircraft carriers, to go down the Suez Canal to combat them. An English Admiral said they are going to punish the Hutias severely by knocking out their navy and airfields. Turkey has warned Syria to stay out of the fray. Tensions are mounting between the Saudis and Iran, and even the Somalians want to get into the picture. The Saudis are very nervous about the events unfolding in the Middle East and have sent their ambassador to the U.S. to meet with the other leaders at the UN. They may have to really increase their oil production if Iran is not in the market.

Pierre and I went to our home base in Paris, just in time for a great dinner that Suzanne had cooked up. Everyone was talking all at once about all the events happening. Lots of rumors flying around.

Gbezx called and told me to come down to the underworld, as Lucifer wants to have us join in a meeting in the situation room. I took the elevator down and met Gbezx in his office. We went out and both rode winged Devils down to the room. This is the same room we had been in earlier. There were perhaps 30 humans in the room, and Lucifer was up front. He asked for comments from the group for their opinion on the ongoing events in the upper world.

One of the lady attendees said she wondered what the election of the new incoming president of the U.S. would affect the outcome. Some of the NATO countries are very nervous and holding strategy meetings amongst themselves now. The citizens are scrambling around, trying to decide what might be the safest country to go to. Relocation companies are cropping up with very expensive plans that only the wealthy can afford. Their brochures show residents in South America, New Zealand, Australia, Africa, Iceland, and some of the small islands around the world.

A man said, "You don't want to go to any of the countries that have nuclear bombs or a country close to that country." Another man felt that an all-out war will break out soon between Russia and Ukraine, with Russia using limited nuclear warheads. This may force the hands of Britain, France, and the U.S. to retaliate.

Another lady said, "India and Pakistan, who have their border issues, will be on high alert. North Korea may join Russia in action against the NATO countries." A man said, "It is hard to know what China may decide, but it's very possible they will attack Taiwan with all the other confusion and countries and war."

One lady said it was really going to be difficult to plan strategy now, and maybe it would be best to hold off and see what happens. Quite a few other participants agreed that waiting might be the best tactic. One man said that different countries are worried about how they will feed their populace, and some are closing borders. There were several comments and questions that went on for another 3 hours. At the end of the meeting, Lucifer thanked everyone for their input and said that his council will consider some of the ideas that were offered here.

Gbezx told me he had a meeting with Lucifer, so for now, I should go back to my home base in France. I took the elevator back up, and Louis greeted me. We went into the apartment and joined the others in the living room. I gave them a brief lecture on what had transpired in the big meeting, and everyone had their thoughts and opinions. Suzanne cooked Oso Buco, which was outstanding. She said it literally meant "hole in the bone." She had a nice selection of sautéed vegetables and lemon pie for dessert.

Silvia said she wanted to talk to me, so she went over to the couch and sat down. She said her sister-in-law was very sick with cancer. Silvia said she and her brother Frank lived in Rockingham, Australia, a town just south of Perth that was on the coast on the western side of the country. She had gotten permission from Gbezx to go down and visit her sister-in-law, and she wondered if I would go with her. I said, "Sure, let me contact Gbezx." She said she already had, and it was okay for me to go and take off a week. She said it is difficult to get airfare out of Paris, but one of Gbezx's staff had arranged a flight in two days. The temperature in Perth was about 70 degrees, so we packed light. We boarded the plane in first class and had seats side by side.

Silvia said she really is having thoughts about continuing to work as one of Lucifer's agents. She had served faithfully for several years, and it is getting too stressful. She said she liked Australia, although it is very hot in the summer. She had visited her brother some years back, and the people were so friendly and relaxed—kind of like a small-town atmosphere. Her brother was an investor in an opal mine and a rancher, and had a comfortable income. Gbezx had told her one time that Lucifer gives out generous retirement plans for faithful employees, so she wouldn't have to worry about living expenses. She asked me how I felt about retiring. I said, "Well, I haven't been working for Lucifer for as long as you have." She said, "That's true, however you've gone on some dangerous missions that should make up for the time spent. In fact, that may be a reason for him not to let you go, as you have a talent for solving problems." I said, "Well, let's see what happens on our vacation here."

Her brother Frank picked us up at Perth Airport. He was a tall, pleasant red-haired man and was dressed in shorts and a T-shirt. It was about 95 degrees, so Silvia and I changed into lighter clothes. We loaded up in his Range Rover and headed south to Rockingham. I asked Frank what the population was in Perth, and he said it was over 2 million, while Rockingham had about 15,000. It was a pleasant drive down the coast. We saw a lot of red kangaroos and a few rare grey kangaroos. They compete with farmers' stock and can be a nuisance. They thin them out occasionally. They are the national animal, revered by many, and are on coins and stamps. Some of them came over to the edge of the road looking for handouts.

We went into Rockingham, and it had the small-town charm, with a number of smaller, older commercial buildings with stores on the first floor and living quarters on the second floor. It had the usual fast food chain stores, including McDonald's. We went to Frank's favorite restaurant for a nice steak and a local beer. I could tell that Silvia was relaxed, and I felt it too. I asked Frank how business was, and he said they had just made a big hit at the opal mine and were very excited about the find. Silvia had told him we both worked for a Canadian stockbroker and that I did a lot of traveling for the company, while she worked in the office.

We finished our meal, and I was surprised at how reasonable the cost was. We headed out to Frank's ranch, which was about 10 miles out of Rockingham. Their main house was a large, single-story ranch-style building with outbuildings, including a barn and various others. He raised about 600 Hereford cattle, which the climate was good for, on about 1,000 hectares of land, he said. He had a manager-ranch hand who lived in one of the other large houses with his family, and his two 20-year-old sons, Ron and George, also worked on the ranch. Their sister, Nancy, was the housekeeper and cook for Frank and Sally.

We went to the large living room, which was decorated in an early western motif. Sally, Silvia's sister-in-law, was in bed, and her care nurse, who was sitting in a chair next to the bed, introduced herself as Sonia and was from the Philippines. She got up from the chair and brought in another one for me to sit in. Sally's voice was very weak, and she seemed to be in pain. Silvia gave her a big hug and told her how sorry she was, then held her hand.

After a while, Sally went to sleep, so we went out and joined Frank in his den. They talked about Sally's condition, and Frank said she doesn't have long to live. Frank asked us if we wanted to take a walk to see some of the ranch. We went to the barn, and outside of it, there were six beautiful horses. He said we could go riding tomorrow if we wanted. We both agreed immediately. From there, we went into the barn, which was full of all kinds of ranching and riding equipment. We went to the pigpen, which had three large sows and maybe 20 other pigs of various ages. He said, "We'll have fresh bacon for breakfast tomorrow, as we butchered a pig about a week ago, and it's been smoked."

Next was the chicken coop, with maybe 50 chickens, so we'd also have fresh eggs. There was a very large barn-like structure with open sides that was full of baled alfalfa hay that he fed to the livestock at certain times of the year. There was a pond that had ducks and geese around it. There was also a nice vegetable garden and a greenhouse. Frank said he got his water from a deep well. We headed back into the house and went to Sally's bedroom, but she was still asleep. Frank asked if we wanted an adult cocktail, so we went to his den. He turned on the TV, and on the news, it was showing turmoil in Syria, with rebels taking over some of the cities. This was making Turkey very concerned, as they backed Assad, the dictator. There was also an uprising in South Korea. Frank said, "It looks like the whole world is falling apart." Silvia and I exchanged looks.

Frank told Silvia her bedroom was down the hall on the left, and mine was on the right. After a good night's sleep, we were awakened with Nancy singing, "Wakey, wakey, eggs and bakey!" A great cup of very hot coffee was on the table. We had toast, our choice of eggs, thick bacon, and hash brown potatoes. Silvia was dressed in tight jeans and a nice white blouse that was very attractive. We went out to the barn and picked out our sized riding boots. Ron and George had saddled up the horses, a spirited brown mare for Silvia and a gentler calico stallion for me. Frank rode his big black stallion. We headed out from the farm buildings with Frank leading. Silvia was an accomplished horsewoman from another life. We rode for a couple of hours, and it was very pleasant as the temperature was only about 85 degrees.

We went to the barn, unsaddled, and walked the horses around a bit to cool them off, then wiped them down. I told Silvia I could get used to this, and she just smiled. Over lunch, Frank told us about a friend of his who gives boat rides to see the big saltwater crocs. These crocodiles can grow to 23 feet or so and weigh 2,500 lbs. He asked if we wanted to take the tour. We said, "What the heck, may never get another opportunity." So, after breakfast the next morning, we loaded up in Frank's Range Rover and headed to the coast. We went to the marina, where we met his friend Bill, who was a big-boned, bald-headed guy of about 6 feet and looked in prime condition. He had the typical wide-brimmed Aussie hat. His boat was a center console, 25-foot open fiberglass model with twin 100-horse outboards. He had a shotgun in a holder attached to the console, and Bill had a .357 Magnum revolver in a side holster.

Bill explained that we would go up some of the island bayous, of which there were many, and cruise along the shore. Many of the crocs would lay along the banks sunning themselves. We might see a few in the water, he said. We went by one beach that had about four crocs in the 12-foot range looking out at the water. We saw several of them as we cruised along, but no real big ones. We rounded a bend, and there were two big guys, about maybe 23 feet or so long. They were about 100 feet from us. As we cruised along slowly, I was up in the bow taking pictures when, all of a sudden, the boat hit something submerged and stopped abruptly, throwing me into the water. Both big crocs slid down the bank and headed over to us. One went to the left side and tried to get into the boat. Silvia began hitting it on the head with one of the oars, and Bill shot the croc with his revolver in the head several times. The other croc came after me, and as it opened its huge jaw, Frank pushed the other oar in its mouth, holding it off me. I was able to pull myself up into the boat with no time to spare, as the croc bit down on the oar, threw it to the side, and lunged for me. Bill grabbed the shotgun and pumped three rounds of double-0 buckshot into its head. "Wow, that was close."

Bill was able to back the boat off the obstruction we had hit. He said, "Hold on, guys, as I'm going to turn around fast." We went for maybe 40 or 50 feet, and he stopped the boat. We all breathed a sigh of relief. We all talked at once, and Bill said to me, "You are very lucky, as you would have been a goner if the croc had grabbed your leg or any part of you. And good job, Frank, in holding him off until I could shoot him. Let me load the guns just in case we need them again." Bill said he had never had this happen before. Silvia said, "Well, we sure got our money's worth of excitement for the day." I was, of course, sopping wet. Frank said, "You're fortunate; it's a warm day." Silvia chipped in, "You needed a bath anyway." I said, "Thanks, Silvia. Do you want to go for a swim?" Bill got four beers out of the cooler, and they really tasted good.

We headed back to the marina and Bill's slip. Bill said, "There's a small café that has good food just a short walk from his dock, and he'll treat because of the close call." We took the last table available; the waitress brought me a towel to sit on. We ordered a beer and a special lunch sandwich, which was delicious. After lunch, we said our goodbyes to Bill and loaded up in Frank's SUV and headed home. Frank asked us if we had thought about getting married. Silvia said, "Well, we've tossed it around a little bit." He asked, "Why don't you two buy a second home down here? You could rent it out and have a place to live when you retire. Prices are low now, so some good purchases are available, starting at about $300,000 USD. I have a friend who is a real estate broker who could find you a good deal." I said, "We'll certainly give that some thought."

Frank asked if we wanted to see the opal mine, and we said, "For sure!" So the next morning, we headed out on a paved road and then turned off onto a bumpy dirt road. We went for about an hour and then came up to the mining area. There was a mine opening about six feet in diameter. Opals are often found in small nodules, and the opal is extracted from them. It's tedious work, as they carefully dig the walls of the shaft and dig boreholes and trenches. They follow veins of opal. Two of Frank's workers, Bill and Tom, were in the shaft, which was maybe 45 feet deep. They were using small pick hammers and chisels and were working on the sides and ceiling. They had a generator running outside the mouth of the shaft to provide lighting. They were not employees but were paid based on the stones they extracted. They had a profit split worked out by their attorneys. They had a couple of good veins they were following, and they excitedly showed us a number of the stones they had accumulated. They told Frank, "It looks like we'll pay for our month's expenses out of one day's digs!"

They had a tent they lived in during the week, and then on the weekend, one would go back to his home in town, then they would rotate the next week. They had to have someone there to guard the mine, or goons would come and rip them off. We unloaded two 5-gallon cans of water and groceries from Frank's SUV. It was lunchtime, so Bill cooked up some steaks, and we had great steak sandwiches, potato chips, and almost-cold beer.

About that time, there was a group of camels that went by. Silvia and I both said, "What the hell are camels doing out here?" Frank explained that way back when, in the early days, the Aussies imported a number of them with their handlers to transport goods from settlement to settlement. They could go for five days without water, which horses or mules couldn't match. The government estimates there are over 1 million wild camels wandering around Australia. Bill and Tom said they needed to get back to work and gave Frank a bag of opals to take back and put in the safe at his house. So, we headed back to Frank's place.

Frank asked if we wanted to experience another adventure. Silvia said, "What is it first? Not more croc ventures, I hope!" Frank laughed and said, "No, I have another friend who owns an air service in Perth, and I can get him to take us for a ride out to the outback in a helicopter. There is a very large sheep ranch with thousands of acres, and now it's shearing time. The herders round them up and herd them into the shearing sheds. You'll be surprised at what they ride."

We got back and went in to see how Sally was doing. She seemed better and told us the doctor had put her on some other medicine. We all expressed how wonderful that was. We had a nice meal and an after-dinner cocktail. Frank said he had called his friend, and we needed to meet him at the airport about 10 a.m. the next day.

We drove through the airport back to where his friend Mike parked his fleet. Mike was of medium height, a trim man who looked to be in very good shape. The four of us loaded into a jet helicopter that Mike said was a fast machine, and away we went due east. He called all of us "Maties."

After about a 30-minute ride, we came across a huge flock of sheep. Herding them along were five people on motorcycles. They really kicked up the dust. They were getting close to the shearing sheds and were corralled in the holding pens. "Wow," I said, "What happened to the cowboy on their horse?" Mike said the bikes are much faster and very maneuverable.

Mike said he knew the sheepman owner and asked if we would like to go down and watch the shearing. We all said yes. Mike called the owner, and he told Mike to put the helicopter down about half a mile away and that he would send a van to pick us up.

Up at the shearing shed was very interesting. There were six corrals leading into the shed. Australian Collies would bring one sheep at a time to be sheared, the shearer would grab the sheep, set it down on its tail, and the electric razors would start buzzing. It was amazing how fast each sheep could be sheared. They had a contest to see how many sheep each shearer could do in a certain time. The first prize was $1000 AUD, second was $500 AUD, and third was $250 AUD. This was on top of the fee the shearers would receive for each one done. There was a second man in each shed who would bag up the wool and put it aside. The dog would run the sheared sheep out to the pen and then bring another one in very fast to the shearer. There is a feeling that these are some of the world's smartest dogs.

We sat in small bleachers to watch the action. They handed out cold Aussie beers to all of us, and they were very good. The older retired dogs were given to neighbors and friends, and you had to pass a test to get one. There was a backlog of people on a waiting list for them.

After visiting local people for a while, Mike said, "Are you ready to move on?" which we did, and we loaded up in the helicopter. We flew back to Perth, and one of Mike's employees started refueling it and checking out the mechanics. Mike said, "The machine is very fast, but it really gobbles up the fuel." We said our goodbyes to Mike, and I asked if we could pay for expenses. He turned me down and said it was a pleasure meeting us.

We loaded up in Frank's Range Rover and headed back home. We stopped by the side of the road and watched a group of wild kangaroos go by. A couple of males were boxing to determine who would be the dominant male. The fight went on for a while, then broke up, and they went their way.

We got back, and Frank said, "We're going to have a big Outback steak Aussie style," so he got the BBQ fired up. We hung around watching him and drinking beer. The meal was outstanding, and the steak melted in your mouth. It was off one of his cattle. After dinner, Frank turned on the TV to see what fun stuff was happening in the world. There was big turmoil in Syria with different factions vying for power, the Turks were battling with Kurds, Israel had two battles in the South and North, Russia was gaining ground in the West of Ukraine as they put more North Korean troops online, and thousands had been killed. There were lots of opinions and hand-wringing by UN members. "What to do, what to do?"

Silvia and I decided to go take a walk. The temperature was perfect, and it was a beautiful evening. Several issues came up. Silvia asked me if I had thought anymore about us getting married. I said, "Yes, I have, and I don't think I could find anyone better suited than you for a wife." I asked if she really thought she could put up with me, and she said she thought so. "We've been through a lot together without much friction so far."

We stopped to have a big kiss. She asked what I thought about moving down here to Australia. I said, "We may have to petition Lucifer. There is a base of operation in Perth with an elevator where we could go down to Hades if requested by Gbezx." Silvia said she would like to semi-retire from service, and I said I had thought about that as well. "We could maybe serve part-time. We could ask Frank about what property is available and what area to look at. We could get all the money we would need from Lucifer to purchase."

A Promise for the Future

At breakfast, we told Frank our thoughts and asked if he could introduce us to his real estate broker friend so we could see the lay of the land. Frank called his friend Leo and told him about our situation. Leo said he could come out to the ranch tomorrow around 10:00 a.m. and we could chat.

The next morning, Leo came to the house. He was an athletic type with red curly hair and a mustache, and had a pleasant personality. We sat at the big wood dining table, and he started asking questions like, "Did we want acreage, like a small ranch? Live in town in a single-family residence? How large of square footage? How about condo living, etc.?"

We said, if it isn't too much trouble, we would like to maybe see a sampling of all of the above, as we have no idea what we are looking for. He asked us what price range worked for us. Silvia and I exchanged glances, and I said, "We have access to money."

Frank asked him to show us maybe properties close to him to start, maybe a small ranchito. Leo said he would go back to his office to do research and then would call us later to go see them.

After Leo had left, Frank said, "Another thing we could do is I could sell you some land off the road we came in on, and you could build a house." Well, we said, "That's an idea." We called Leo and made an appointment for the next day. He came and picked us up, and we headed out to some small ranches that had houses and outbuildings on them.

We kind of liked one that was only a few miles from Frank's, but it was a fixer-upper, so we passed on it. We drove into Rockingham and looked at a couple of houses. A $640,000 AU = $400,000 US. A 3-bedroom house was $600,000 to $800,000 AU.

We had lunch at a nice Aussie steakhouse. Then we went to see a few more of the town, which was charming with a small-town feeling.

Back home at Frank's that evening, we told him what we had seen. He said, "Tomorrow, let's go down the road about a mile, and I will show you a parcel of land I own that is next to the road."

The next day, we mounted up on the horses and rode down the road a mile or so to the parcel he told us about. He had bought 100 acres of land from his neighbor. He said, "I could deed off a couple of acres to you on the corner. I would make you a very fair deal. I have a good friend who is a very honest contractor who could build you a nice custom house and maybe some outbuildings if you wanted."

Silvia and I exchanged looks and told Frank we would like to think about it. We had been there about 10 days, and we told Frank we needed to get back to work, so we really liked his idea. He asked us if we needed money, and we said, "No, we have access to funds."

I called Gbezx and told him we were coming back. He said, "When you get there, you need to come down to see me."

So, we packed our bags, and Frank had one of his ranch hands drive us to the airport in Perth. After a long airplane ride, we arrived in Paris and went to our base. I had dinner with Silvia, Mary, Louis, Pierre, and Suzanne, and then the next morning went down to Hades.

I met Gbezx at his office, and I told him what activities we had done. He said, "Let's go see the Master," so we went to his opulent office. He said, "There is a lot of friction in the world, and they are monitoring it closely. They have an assignment for me in Saudi Arabia and Iran, and Gbezx will fill me in."

He asked me how Silvia and I have been getting along, so I told him that Silvia and I wanted to get married, and if possible, semi-retire in some fashion and live in Australia. I told him about Frank's offer to sell us some land, and we could build a home on it.

"Hmm," he said, "Well, this is a surprise. Let me and Gbezx talk it over. You both have served us well, so that's in your favor. Go now with Gbezx."

"Well, David, this is a big surprise," Gbezx said as we walked down to his office. I said, "I can still be on call for your special assignments."

"We will see," he said.

"Here is what is happening with Saudi Arabia and Iran: the current government in Iran is shipping arms down through the Persian Gulf, through the Gulf of Oman, and south through the Arabian Sea to Yemen, and the Houthis are then attacking shipping in the Red Sea."

The Saudis are not happy with this at all and are pressuring France, England, and the US to send more warships to the Red Sea area. Israel has bombed some sites in Iran, and of course, all the countries in the region want the US to step it up. We have a contact in Abu Dhabi in the United Arab Emirates.

Gbezx said he wanted me to go back to France and wait for a week, then fly to Abu Dhabi, where their contact Ali Mukalla would pick me up at the airport. He was waiting for me. He was about average height and wore the Arab robe and headgear. He speaks French and English and has some interesting influential friends in the Royal family as well.

"I was told you were also a good golfer," Ali said. "I would like you to beat one of the arrogant Royal sons, Salan, who thinks he's a big shot with about a 5 handicap. The other son, Mohammad Solamon, is also hooked on the game and is about a 10. I'm a solid 12 myself."

The Saudis are really into golf in a big way, and some very heavy bets are laid down. They have been building some very nice new courses. Gbezx said he would send up $10K to Ali so I would have money to bet on and have some fun with. I also told him you are our troubleshooter and have a high-standing position with Lucifer.

Ali was a pleasant man with a full black beard and in trim shape. He told me to come down to the front outside door the next day about 8 a.m. He said he had us matched up with the assistant golf course pro, Ibrhim, and aides to Salan and Abarham. He said we would need to get to the course early to pick out clubs for me and hit a few practice balls.

As I was going up the elevator, a robed Saudi asked me if I was an American. I said I was, but now in France. He said, "You Americans have ruined the world." I asked, "How so?" He said, "Sticking your nose in other countries' business, like Iraq and other countries." I said, "Yes, I must agree with you, as we have made some big blunders."

We came to his floor, and he said goodbye. Interesting thought, I wondered how many people thought the same way.

After breakfast, I went down and met Ali, and we drove through the heavy traffic to the course. It was designed by the famous golfer Jack Nicklaus and was beautiful. I got my rental clubs, and Ali and I went to the driving range. Ibrhim and Abarkam were there, and Ali introduced me. We hit a bucket of balls, then met them at the clubhouse. They lined us up with caddies, and we decided to walk the course. It was a beautiful day, and we all were really playing well. I finished with a 3-over 75, Ali with an 81, Abarkam with an 80, and Ibrhim with a 78.

Abarkam asked me what we were doing the next day, and Ali asked what he had in mind. He said he would like to pair us up with his boss Salan and maybe Mohammad. Ali and I went to the side, and Ali said, "This would be a great chance to meet some royalty and one of the most influential men in Arabia." Ali asked Abarkam what time, and he said 8 a.m. and he would make all the arrangements.

Ali and I went to his shop where his team and the elevator to Hades were. I met some of his four people, and they were all Arab. They spoke Farsi and some French, and one spoke English. Their job was to stir up problems with the local town people and the ruling class. There was a small group of socialists they worked with.

My job was to meet some of the Royal family or other leaders and try to influence them to cause their enemies, the Iranians, troubles. There was friction between the Sunnis and the Shiites that had gone on for centuries. It was a complete stroke of luck to have a chance to play golf with the Royals. Wow.

The limo took me back to my hotel, and I went to bed early to get ready for the match tomorrow.

The next morning, I went to the course and met Ali. I got a bucket of balls and went over to the driving range where we met Abarkam, and he said it was all set up: Salan, Mohammad, me, and him. Ali would ride along in my cart. A few minutes later, Mohammad and his security guards, and Salan with his, arrived.

Salan shook my hand with a very strong grip. He was about 6 feet tall, had a nicely trimmed black beard, and piercing dark eyes. He was wearing the typical headgear and a short robe. He said to me, "I heard you were a ringer and a scratch player." I laughed and said, "I wish I were."

He asked, "What's your handicap?"

I said, "Probably a 6 or so, and that I was a sporadic player."

Mohammad was about 5'10" and had kind of a weak handshake. He wore about the same clothes as Salan and also had a well-trimmed beard. They were both Crown Princes and brothers.

Salan asked, "Are you a betting man?"

I said, "It depends on the stakes."

I asked them, "Have you ever played Bingo, Bango, Bongo?"

They said, "What in the hell is that?"

I explained, "Okay, Bingo is the 1st on the green, Bango is closest to the hole, and Bongo is the 1st in the hole. This makes it pretty fair to all."

The three of them had a little conference and decided to try it out.

Salan asked, "So how will we bet?"

I said, "We can bet on each of the three B's, say $50 on each one, so you could win $150 on each hole."

Salan said, "Let's make it $100 for each B, $300 each hole. Plus $1,000 for the last total score."

We all agreed that it was fine. In my mind, I decided to try to win $1,000 in B's and then let Salan win the match at the end.

On the 1st hole, Mohammad hit a great drive and was 1st on. Salan hit it closest to the pin, and I was 1st in with a long putt. Our play went back and forth, and all three of the Saudis were having a lot of fun.

"Great game," said Mohammad, and as we were waiting for the players in front of us to clear the course, he called over one of his entourage members to me and asked him to copy down the rules.

We came to the 425 ft par 4, the 17th hole, and Salan was at 4 over par, and I was 4 over. The other two were 10 and 12 over.

Salan said, "Okay, Baker, how about a side bet of $10,000 between the two of us on this last hole?"

I thought that I wanted him to win, but I didn't want to lose that much. So, I said, "That's tempting, but you've had some lucky shots, and I'm starting to fade, so I'll pass on your bet."

He had done well on the Bingo, Bango, Bongo betting, so he said, "Okay, fair enough, let's see who the winner is."

He hit 1st with a nice, straight drive of about 250 yards and was really proud of it. I thought, I'll give him some anxiety, so I blasted one out close to 300 yards, over the top of his.

"Whoee," he said, "Where did that come from?" He looked a little shaken. He hit a 5-iron about 10 yards short of the green. I hit a 9-iron real hard on purpose and went over the green. He hit a wedge up on the green, about 10 feet from the hole, and was lying 3. I hit a sand wedge up to about 25 feet from the hole and was also lying 3.

I putted 1st and missed the hole by 1 foot, lying 4. He putted it in for a 4, and I putted in for a 5, so he beat me by one stroke. He was so happy, he jumped up and down, and his entourage was clapping and cheering, as well as some other people who had heard about the match and came to watch.

We shook hands, and he gave me a hug. He had shot his best round. We were shaking the other players' hands and talking about what a good match it was. We figured out the money on the three B's, and I won $50 after I paid Salan for the $1,000 final bet. Perfect, I thought.

He invited us all over to his mansion for tea and conversation.

Salan, Abarkam, Ali, and I were driven in his bulletproof limo to his vast estate. Mohammad had to leave us for another commitment. We drove past a wonderful garden and stopped in front of the mansion. It was magnificent. His butler led us back to the outdoor lounge, and we sat down on large pillows. A servant brought tea, water, and some dates that were very tasty.

"So, Mr. Baker, what brings you here to our country?" Salan asked.

"Well," I said, "I represent some wealthy patrons who are very concerned about what is happening in the world, particularly Iran. They know that you Saudis are no friends with the Iranians, and we want to strategize with you to nullify their standing in the world and military capabilities. What I bring to you today is just an opening gesture of future cooperation."

"Do your people have any plans?" Salan asked.

"Not as such," I replied. "We see ourselves as background implementers to help you. Maybe even using our influence with the Americans, Israelis, and perhaps others to strike Iran's facilities."

"Hmmm, very interesting, Mr. Baker." He thought for a minute and then said, "I will need to bring this before our Council. These are dangerous times, as you know, and we need to proceed slowly. Let's do this: I will present your offer to our people, and I may ask you to come back to speak to them. So, Mr. Baker, I thank you for the great game; you brought the best out of me. I will contact Ali when we want to meet with you again."

He motioned for one of his staff to come over and told them to call my hotel and arrange their best suite for me, putting it on his account. "It may take a week or so for me to meet with my people," he said. We said our goodbyes, and Ali and I left for my hotel. He would drop me off a few blocks from his home base. "I'll send a car to pick you up the next morning at 7 a.m.," he said. "Then we can go to breakfast and talk things over."

I told him I would need to go back down and inform Gbezx and Lucifer about the situation with the Saudis once we were finished.

The deluxe suite was unlike anything I'd seen before. It had a small swimming pool, a spa, and a masseuse who asked if I wanted treatment now or after dinner. "After dinner will be fine," I replied. The butler gave me a menu and recommended the lamb chops, so I chose the vegetables I wanted to go with it. He then asked if I wanted a Cuban cigar and a snifter of brandy, and I agreed, saying I would have them after the massage.

He told me he would call up the masseuse after my dinner. I took a nice shower in an 8-foot by 8-foot marble shower, put on a plush robe, and laid down on the big bed. The butler came in with my meal and set it down on a table that overlooked the city. I was on the 98th floor. The dinner was outstanding, and the chops melted in my mouth.

About 15 minutes later, the masseuse came in with her table and gave me a very relaxing massage. The butler then asked if I wanted my cigar and brandy. "Wow, this is living!" I thought to myself.

After a great night's sleep, I swam a few laps, jumped in the jacuzzi, got dressed, and met Ali out front. We went to his favorite restaurant for an Arab breakfast, which was interesting. I told him about the hotel experience, and he laughed. "Boy, that's really roughing it!" he joked.

We went to his base, said our goodbyes, and I took the elevator down to the underworld, as they called it. I met with Lucifer, and Gbezx said, "You are lucky and good."

"I'd always rather be lucky than good," I replied.

Lucifer said, "We need to think about what we can offer the Saudis in strategy. They have plenty of military arms, and they have plenty of money. They are conservative, perhaps a little timid. They do have an abundance of oil, which they've used in the past to negotiate with other countries. Iran also has oil reserves. If the Saudis were able to get the U.S., Israel, or someone else to attack Iran's oil fields, then the Saudis could raise prices on their oil and have more negotiating leverage."

Gbezx said, "Let's think along those lines and maybe have another large meeting like we've had in the past, which often brings up good ideas."

"Good idea," Lucifer said. "Why don't you have your assistant set it up right away?"

I went back up to our base in Paris. I shared some of the highlights of the recent events with the others. Mary said, "You're sure making friends in high places; pretty soon, you won't even talk to us."

"Don't worry about that," I said. "I'm a fairly humble guy."

They all laughed at that. Gbezx said that Ali had some information for me and that I should call him. Ali said the Saudis had called him and that they would need some time to study our proposal and wanted to tell our employers that they really appreciated the gesture of cooperation.

Gbezx asked me to come down and brief Lucifer and him about what had unfolded in Arabia.

I went over everything that had transpired. Lucifer said, "It seems like it's a waiting game with them as well. The Saudis are known for procrastination and moving slowly. We have some business here to attend to. Gbezx and I have talked and thought about you and Silvia's proposal to semi-retire, move to Australia, get married, and acquire property to live on. We've decided that if you, Mr. Baker, would agree to come back and help us if an issue arises that requires your talent, we would be grateful."

I said, "That's very nice of you, and I will agree."

"We will promote Mary to take Silvia's position. Let Gbezx know when you need funds to purchase property."

Gbezx said, "Go pick up Silvia and your belongings, and head to Australia."

I went up to France to our station and told everyone the news. There were some teary eyes and hugs all around. Silvia made airline reservations, called her Uncle Frank, and we packed our clothes. The next day, Pierre drove us to the airport.

One of Frank's ranch hands met us at the airport, and we drove out to the ranch. We told Frank our plans and that we would like to take him up on his offer for the land sale. Silvia also said that we wanted to get married. Frank said, "Let me know when, and I'll set it up with our pastor."

We had a simple wedding a few days later at the small church in Rockingham. Frank said that we could stay with him in their guest bedroom until our house could be built.

I called Gbezx on my special phone and told him what had happened. He said he was pleased and to call once a month. We really enjoyed Frank's hospitality, and he enjoyed our company.

Well, so far, everything is calm and peaceful.

www.ingramcontent.com/pod-product-compliance
Lightning Source LLC
Chambersburg PA
CBHW041739300726
48978CB00006B/165